My Weirdest School #2

Ms. Cuddy Is Nutty!

Dan Gutman

Pictures by
Jim Paillot

HARPER
An Imprint of HarperCollinsPublishers

To Emma

My Weirdest School #2: Ms. Cuddy Is Nutty!
Text copyright © 2015 by Dan Gutman
Illustrations copyright © 2015 by Jim Paillot

Library of Congress Control Number: 2014949454
ISBN 978-0-06-228424-2 (pbk.) — ISBN 978-0-06-228425-9 (lib. bdg.)

Typography by Aurora Parlagreco
18 19   CG/LSCH   10 9 8 7 6 5 4 3
❖
First Edition

Contents

How Do You Like Them Apples?

My name is A.J. and I hate it when my school gets attacked by monsters.

I should explain.

It all started the other day when our new teacher, Mr. Cooper, came flying into the room. And I do mean *flying*! Mr. Cooper thinks he's a superhero. But he's not a very good one, because he knocked over the garbage can and fell on the floor. Stuff spilled all over the place.

We all ran over to help him up. Mr. Cooper had a black plastic bag in his hand and a letter *A* on his cape.

"It is I," he announced. "Apple Man!"

"Apple Man?" asked Ryan and Michael.

"Whoever heard of a superhero named Apple Man?" asked Alexia, who rides a skateboard all the time.

"Today we're going to learn about apples," said Mr. Cooper.

"Why?" asked Neil, who we call the nude kid even though he wears clothes.

"Because it's part of the Common Core!" said Mr. Cooper. "Get it?"

Nobody got it. But Mr. Cooper didn't care. He took some apples out of the bag and passed them around.

"When I was a kid, we used to say 'An apple a day keeps the doctor away,'" Mr. Cooper told us.

"You threw apples at doctors?" I asked. Then everybody laughed even though I didn't say anything funny.

"Did you know there are seven *thousand* kinds of apples grown all over the world?" Mr. Cooper asked us. "But only *one* is native to North America—the crabapple."*

"I know something about apples," said Andrea Young, this annoying girl with curly brown hair. "If you put an apple in water, it won't sink. Apples have a lot of air in them."

"Very good, Andrea!" said Mr. Cooper.

Andrea fist-bumped her friend Emily, the big crybaby. Then she smiled the smile that she smiles to let everybody know that

---

*I bet you never thought that this book would be EDU-CATIONAL!

she knows something nobody else knows. She thinks she is *so* smart. Why can't a truck full of apples fall on her head?

Mr. Cooper told us it was time for math.

"If there are six apples on a table and you take away four of them, how many do you have?" Mr. Cooper asked.

Andrea was waving her hand in the air like she needed to be rescued from a desert island.

"Two apples!" she said. "Because six minus four is two." Then she made her smiley smile again.

"No," said Mr. Cooper. "If there are six apples on a table and you take away four of them, you have four of them, of course.

You just took four of them away!"

"B-but . . . but . . ."

We all laughed because Andrea said "but," which sounds like "butt" even though it only has one *t*.

Ha-ha! Ha-ha! Nah-nah-nah boo-boo on Andrea.

Mr. Cooper taught us lots of interesting stuff about apples. Did you know that gravity was discovered when an apple fell on some guy's head? Me neither.

That's when the most amazing thing in the history of the world happened. The morning announcements came over the loudspeaker.

Well, that's not the amazing part,

because the morning announcements come over the loudspeaker *every* morning. The amazing part was what happened after that.

I'm not going to tell you what it was.

Okay, okay, I'll tell you.

But you have to read the next chapter. So nah-nah-nah boo-boo on you.

A Surprise Guest

Our school secretary, Mrs. Patty, does the announcements every morning. We pledge the allegiance, and then she tells us the weather, what's for lunch, and who has birthdays that day. It's pretty boring.

At the end of today's announcements, Mrs. Patty said, "All students and teachers, please report to the all-purpose room for a surprise assembly."

We had to walk single file a million hundred miles to the all-purpose room. Mr. Cooper made us sit boy-girl-boy-girl so we wouldn't sit next to anybody we liked. I had to sit between Andrea and Emily.

Our principal, Mr. Klutz, climbed up on the stage. He has no hair at all. I mean *none*. He used to have hair, but it fell out or something. Everybody was buzzing.

Well, not really. People don't buzz. Bees buzz. It would be weird if people buzzed like bees. But we were all talking. Mr. Klutz held up his hand and made a peace sign, which means "shut up."

"Thank you," he said. "We have a *very* special guest at Ella Mentry School today."

We all buzzed some more. And you'll never believe who walked out on the stage at that moment.

Nobody! Because somebody *rolled* out on the stage . . . in a wheelchair.

It was Mrs. Ella Mentry!

Ella Mentry is a really old lady who used to teach at our school a million hundred years ago. She must have been a good teacher, because after she retired the school was named after her. There's a big sign on the grass out front that says ELLA MENTRY SCHOOL.

One time when Mrs. Mentry came to our school, things got out of hand and there was a food fight. Pickle chips and

meatballs and burritos and Tater Tots were flying through the air. It was cool.

We gave Mrs. Mentry a standing ovation. A standing ovation is when everybody gets up from their seats and claps their hands. When you stand up and clap your hands, it's a lot better than when you just sit there and clap your hands. Nobody knows why.

At first I wasn't going to stand up. But all the teachers stood up. Then a few kids stood up. And then a lot *more* kids stood up. And then I felt like I would look like a dork if I *didn't* stand up. So I stood up.

While we were clapping, Mr. Klutz dragged out a big, white piece of cardboard.

It was about the size of a door.

"Mrs. Mentry has brought a gift for the school today," Mr. Klutz announced.

"She's giving us a *door*?" I asked. "What do we need a door for? We have plenty of doors."

"It's not a *door*, Arlo!" Andrea said, rolling her eyes. She calls me by my real name because she knows I don't like it. "It's a *check*. Mrs. Mentry is donating *money* to our school, dumbhead!"

I wanted to say something mean to Andrea, but all I could think of was "Your *face* looks like a door."

In my head, I was wondering why Mrs. Mentry's check was so *big*. My parents use checks, and their checks are about the size of a dollar bill. Why would anybody need to have a check the size of a *door*? I can imagine how big Mrs. Mentry's wallet is.

Mr. Klutz handed the microphone to Mrs. Mentry.

"Thank you for that wonderful welcome," she said. "I will always have a special place in my heart for this school. And to show my appreciation, I would like to give this to you."

Mr. Klutz turned the check around so we could see the other side. This is what it looked like. . . .

WHAT!?

"A million dollars!" I shouted.

"A million dollars!!" shouted Alexia.

"A million dollars!!!!" shouted Ryan.

In case you were wondering, we were all shouting, "A million dollars."

Everybody started yelling and screaming and shrieking and hooting and hollering and generally freaking out. You should have been there!

A Hundred Thousand Pizzas

Nobody could believe Ella Mentry was actually giving the school *a million dollars*. Man, that lady must have a *ton* of money to be giving away so much of it. No wonder she needs such big checks. There are a lot of zeroes in a million.

We gave Mrs. Mentry another standing

ovation. Then Mr. Klutz made the shut-up peace sign again and we all got quiet.

"We can't thank you enough, Mrs. Mentry," he said. "But now we have a problem. What are we going to do with this money?"

That's a problem? If you ask me, a problem is when you have *no* money at all.

"I'll spend it for you!" shouted our librarian, Mrs. Roopy. Everybody laughed.

"Tell you what I'm going to do," Mr. Klutz said. "We're going to have a contest to decide what to do with the money."

"Oooooh!" everybody oohed.

"Go back to your classrooms and think of some ideas for what we should do with the million dollars," Mr. Klutz told us. "The class that comes up with the best idea will be the first to use whatever we buy with the money. I'll announce the winning class at the end of the day."

We walked a million hundred miles back to our classroom.

"So," Mr. Cooper said when we were seated, "what do you think we should buy with the million dollars?"

"Pizza!" Ryan shouted. "We should have a giant pizza party for the whole school!"

"Yeah!" everybody yelled.

Ryan should be in the gifted and talented program for coming up with *that* idea. Who doesn't like pizza?

"Do you know how many pizzas you

can buy with a million dollars?" Mr. Cooper asked.

He went to the board and wrote the number *1,000,000* on it. He told us a pizza costs about ten dollars. Then he divided 1,000,000 by 10.

"A hundred thousand pizzas!" shouted Andrea.

"That's a lot of pizza!" said Michael.

"I can only eat one or two slices," said Emily.

"Me too," said Alexia.

"We can freeze the rest for leftovers," said Neil. "That's what we do at home."

"May I ask where we will put all that leftover pizza?" asked Mr. Cooper.

"I know," said Alexia. "We can buy a thousand refrigerators!"

"Yeah!" everybody shouted.

"And where are we going to *put* a thousand refrigerators?" asked Mr. Cooper.

"In the playground!" Michael said.

"Yeah!" everybody shouted.

"As long as we're getting all those refrigerators," said Neil, "let's buy a million dollars' worth of ice cream. I like ice cream better than pizza."

"Yeah!" everybody shouted.

"Why don't we just buy a million dollars' worth of candy?" I suggested. "Then we won't need any refrigerators."

"Yeah!" everybody shouted.

We were coming up with some really good ideas. I was sure that our class would win the contest.

"I hate to tell you this," said Mr. Cooper, "but Ella Mentry did not give us a million dollars to buy junk food. She wants us to buy something *useful* for the school. We need to think outside the box."

I didn't see any boxes around. If I was

in a box, I know what I would be thinking about—how to get out of the box.

"We could buy a racing car with a million dollars," suggested Michael.

"Maybe we could buy a football team," suggested Neil.

"How about a skate park?" Alexia suggested.

"Why not give the million dollars to a school that doesn't have any money?" suggested Emily.

"*Our* school doesn't have any money!" I told her.

"Well, we have money *now*," said Emily. "We have a million dollars."

"But if we gave the million dollars to a school that doesn't have any money," I told her, "then *we* would be a school that doesn't have any money again!"

"Maybe we should put the money in the bank," suggested Little Miss Perfect. "Then we could watch it grow."

"Banks are boring," I said.

"Well, what if we did something

educational with the money," suggested Mr. Cooper.

Ugh. He said the *E* word.

"Educational stuff is boring," I said.

"Well, A.J.," said Mr. Cooper. "What is *not* boring to you?"

I tried to think of something that isn't boring. It was hard, because most stuff is boring.

"TV," I finally said. "TV isn't boring."

That's when I got the greatest idea in the history of the world.

"I know!" I said. "We should buy one of those big flat-screen TVs for our class. That would be cool!"

"Yeah!" everybody shouted.

"A flat-screen TV doesn't cost a million dollars," Mr. Cooper told us. "For a million dollars we could buy a whole TV *station*."

"Well," I said, "then we should buy our own TV station."

"That's it!" shouted Mr. Cooper. "A.J., you're a *genius*!"*

---

*Hey, how come this book is called *Ms. Cuddy Is Nutty!* but it doesn't have anybody named Ms. Cuddy in it? That's weird.

Boats

I didn't even know you could *buy* your own TV station. But I guess with a million dollars you can buy just about *anything*.

Everybody agreed that my idea was genius and that I should get the Nobel Prize. That's a prize they give out to people who don't have bells.

Well, *almost* everybody agreed. Annoying Andrea had on her mean face. She was mad because I came up with a great idea and she didn't.

Mr. Cooper wrote down my idea and sent it to the office. At the end of the day, just before dismissal, Mr. Klutz made an announcement over the loudspeaker.

"Well, we had a lot of great suggestions for what we should do with the million dollars," he said, "but I could only pick one. So here is my decision—we're going to start our own Ella Mentry School TV station! The winner is Mr. Cooper's class!"

Everybody started yelling and screaming and shrieking and hooting and hollering and generally freaking out.

* * *

Outside school the next morning we were all excited. Some men wearing overalls were carrying giant cameras, computers, lights, and TVs into the school. Somebody said that every class was going to get its own flat-screen TV.

When I got to class, one of those overalls guys was mounting a TV on the wall. That's when we heard Mrs. Patty's voice on the loudspeaker.

"Today is Wednesday," she said. "Blah blah blah blah sunny and breezy outside blah blah blah blah today's lunch will be hot dogs blah blah blah blah we have a birthday—Kerry Frew in first grade blah blah blah . . ."

She went on and on for a million hundred minutes. What a snoozefest. Nobody was listening. But after we pledged the allegiance, Mrs. Patty said something that caught our attention.

"Today will be my last day making the morning announcements," she said. "Starting tomorrow, the announcements will be made over the new Ella Mentry School TV station!"

"Yay!" we all shouted.

"Okay," said Mr. Cooper, "turn to page twenty-three in your math—"

He didn't get the chance to finish his sentence, because you'll never believe who ran through the door at that moment.

Nobody! You can't run through a *door*. Doors are made of wood. But you'll never believe who ran through the door*way*.

It was a lady with dark hair and big eyes.

"My name is Ms. Cuddy," she said.

"To what do we owe the pleasure of your company, Ms. Cuddy?" asked Mr. Cooper.

That's grown-up talk for "What are *you* doing here?"

"Mr. Klutz hired me to help the class start your TV station," Ms. Cuddy said. "I'm a digital media arts teacher."

I never heard of digital media arts, but we were all glad she was here, because none of us knew anything about cameras and lights and microphones. And besides, we would miss math.

"This TV station is going to be *awesome*!" said Ms. Cuddy. "Every class in the school will be able to watch the morning announcements, and people all over town will be able to tune in, too! So your parents will see you on TV."

"Cool!" we all said.

"Now, which one of you is A.J.?" asked Ms. Cuddy.

Everybody looked at me.

"For our first week on the air, *you're* going to be the anchor," said Ms. Cuddy.

"The anchor?" I asked. "Does that mean I get thrown off a boat?"

"No, no," said Ms. Cuddy. "That means you get to read the morning announcements on TV."

"How come Arlo gets to be the anchor?" whined Andrea. "I would make a *great* anchor."

"You would not," I said.

"Would too," said Andrea.

"Not!"

"Too!"

We went back and forth like that for a while.

"The TV station was A.J.'s idea," said Mr. Cooper. "That's why he gets to be the anchor."

I stuck my tongue out at Andrea. Nah-nah-nah boo-boo on her.

"I'm going to be the best anchor in the history of anchors," I announced.

"Well, let's not go overboard, A.J.," said Mr. Cooper.

Why is everybody always talking about being thrown out of boats?

Ms. Cuddy took us to the conference room, where those men with overalls were hammering and sawing and building the scenery for our morning announcements.

There was a flat-screen TV on the wall. The conference room was starting to look like a real TV studio.

Ms. Cuddy told us that somebody would have to operate the camera. Michael volunteered. Alexia asked if she could be the director. Andrea said she would write the scripts. The person in charge of the lights

is called the gaffer, and Ryan got that job. Neil said he would handle the microphones, props, and other stuff. Emily said she would take care of makeup. Ms. Cuddy showed us how to work all the equipment.

"Tomorrow morning," she said, "we're going to make history!"

Making History

We got to school early the next day so we would be ready to do the morning announcements. The conference room looked just like a real TV studio. Ms. Cuddy gave me a fancy jacket and tie to wear so I would look like an anchorman.

Michael, Ryan, and Neil ran around

making sure the equipment was working. Andrea handed me the script she had written.

"Two minutes to airtime!" shouted Alexia, our director.

Ms. Cuddy gathered us all around.

"Okay, this is it, guys," she said. "Our first broadcast. Are you ready to make history?"

"Yeah!" we all replied.

"I can't *hear* you!" said Ms. Cuddy.

"YEAH!" we all replied.

I sat behind the desk and adjusted the mic. Emily ran over and stuck some furry brush in my face.

"Hey, knock it off!" I told her.

"I need to powder your nose," she said. "It's shiny!"

"I don't care," I said. "Leave my nose alone! Get out of here!"

Emily started crying and ran out of the

conference room. What a crybaby.

"One minute!" said Alexia.

There was electricity in the air. Well, not really. If there was electricity in the air, we would get electrocuted.

As I stared at the camera, I felt myself starting to sweat. Every kid in the school would be watching me. My parents would be watching at home. A bunch of strangers would be watching too.

Why had I agreed to do this? I wished we had spent the million dollars on pizza and ice cream and candy. I wanted to run away to Antarctica and go live with the penguins.

"Are you nervous, A.J.?" asked Ms. Cuddy.

"Yeah," I said. "I think I might throw up."

"Good," she replied. "That means you're excited. Remember to speak slowly and clearly."

"Three . . . two . . . one . . . ," said Alexia.

A little red light lit up on top of the camera. I took a deep breath.

"Action!" said Alexia.

"My name is A.J. and here are the morning announcements for Ella Mentry School," I said. "Today is Thursday. The weather outside is cloudy and cold. Today's lunch will be chicken nuggets. We have one birthday. Rocco Garcia in fourth grade turns ten years old today.

Please stand for the Pledge of Allegiance."

Outside the conference room, I could hear lots of kids reciting the pledge.

"Thank you," I said when they were done. "This is A.J., signing off. Have a great Thursday!"

"And . . . *cut*!" shouted Alexia.

The red light on top of the camera went off. Everybody started clapping.

"Nice job, A.J.!" said Ms. Cuddy.

"You nailed it, dude!" said Michael.

That's when the most amazing thing in the history of the world happened. Ms. Cuddy went to turn off the TV, but she must have pushed the wrong button because she changed the channel instead.

Some girl was on the screen. She was sitting at a desk in front of a microphone, and she was wearing a funny hat, fake nose, and glasses.

"This is Morgan Brocklebank," she said, "and this has been the morning announcements from Dirk School."

WHAT?! Dirk School is on the other side of town. We all call it Dork School.

"One last thing before I sign off," Morgan Brocklebank said. "We want to give a special thank-you to Mrs. Ella Mentry, who donated the money for us to start our TV station."

WHAT?!

"Mrs. Mentry gave *them* a million dollars *too*?" shouted Andrea.

"That's not fair!" shouted Neil.

"I thought she only gave the money to *our* school!" shouted Alexia.

Everybody was upset. But one person was more upset than anyone else.

Ms. Cuddy.

More Eyeballs

Ms. Cuddy was staring at the TV with her mouth open. She didn't say anything. But I could tell she was *really* angry. She made both of her hands into fists, and it looked like her eyes were on fire.

"Those dirty, rotten . . ."

She was mumbling to herself. Then she

started shouting.

"How *dare* they start up a TV station at Dirk School the same day we start our TV station? This is *horrible*! I won't stand for it!"

She was really freaking out! I thought she was going to throw something. I had never seen a grown-up get so mad.

That's when Mr. Klutz's voice came over the loudspeaker.

"Great job with the morning announcements, kids!" he said. "I was watching in my office. Terrific, A.J.! And I just heard that fifty-four people in town were watching you at home."

"How many people were watching the

Dirk School morning announcements?" asked Ms. Cuddy.

"Sixty," said Mr. Klutz.

"Noooooo!" shouted Ms. Cuddy as she fell to her knees. She looked like she had just seen the earth destroyed by a meteor.

"I can't believe those Dirk jerks beat us!" she moaned.

"Does it really matter how many people tune in to watch us?" asked Andrea.

"I mean, it's *just* the morning announcements."

Ms. Cuddy jumped to her feet.

"Of *course* it matters!" she shouted. "We are winners at Ella Mentry School, and don't you forget it! Nobody beats us. We're number one! I didn't go to film school for four years to come in *second*!"

She started pacing back and forth.

"We need more eyeballs," she muttered. "How are we going to get more eyeballs?"

That was weird. Why would she want more eyeballs? Aren't two eyeballs enough?*

Ms. Cuddy is nutty.

---

*What would we do with more eyeballs anyway? And where would you get eyeballs? I don't even think you can rent them.

"Do you mean we need more people to watch our morning announcements?" asked Andrea.

"Yes!" Ms. Cuddy replied. "We need to do something tomorrow morning that will blow Dirk School out of the water."

Why is everybody always talking about boats?

"We could get a funny hat and have A.J. put on a fake nose and glasses," suggested Michael.

"No, Dirk already did that," Ms. Cuddy said, still pacing back and forth. "We have to come up with something new and different. A.J., do you have any special talents that nobody else can do?"

"I can make armpit farts," I told her.

"*That's* a special talent?"

"A.J. is good at telling jokes," said Ryan. "He told jokes in the school talent show."

"That might work," said Ms. Cuddy. "A.J., tomorrow morning I want you to come in here with your best jokes."

"Does that mean I don't write the scripts anymore?" asked Andrea.

"You help with the lights tomorrow," Ms. Cuddy told Andrea.

Andrea looked all mad. I stuck out my tongue at her to make her madder. Ha! I would be in front of the camera while she would have to lug lights around. This was the greatest day of my life.

But Seriously

I spent that night practicing my jokes. The next morning, everybody was running around like crazy to get ready. I sat behind the desk. My face felt sweaty. Emily tried to powder my nose, but I told her to leave me alone.

"Okay, let's *do* this thing!" shouted Ms. Cuddy. "Are you ready, A.J.?"

"Yeah!"

"I can't hear you!"

"YEAH!"

"Three . . . two . . . one . . . ," said Alexia.

The red light lit up.

"Action!" said Alexia.

"My name is A.J. and I hate the morning announcements," I said. "Why do we have announcements anyway? We might as well sit at home and tell jokes instead. By the way, speaking of sitting at home, my dad used to work at a calendar factory, but he got fired. Do you know why?"

"Why?" everybody shouted.

"He took too many days off," I said. "Hey, do you know what's bad for your health?"

"What?" everybody shouted.

"Too many birthdays," I said. "What did Earth say to Mars?"

"What?" everybody shouted.

"Get a life!" I said. "And speaking of dead things, do you want some of my old, dead batteries? They're free of charge. But seriously, folks, what did the tie say to the hat?"

"What?" everybody shouted.

"You go on a head. I'll hang around," I said. "Hey, speaking of hanging around, my mom said I was outstanding, because I stand outside a lot. And speaking of being outside, basketball sure is a messy sport, isn't it? The players dribble all over the floor! And speaking of messy things, did you know that watermelons have really fancy weddings? Well, they cantaloupe."

I told a few more jokes, and then Alexia gave me the sign that time was almost up.

"Well, that's our morning announcements for today," I said. "This is A.J., signing off. You stay classy, Ella Mentry students."

"And . . . *cut*!" shouted Alexia.

The red light on top of

the camera turned off.

"Great, A.J.!" said Ms. Cuddy. "I'd like to see Dirk School top *that*!"

She went over to change the channel to the Dirk morning announcements. That girl Morgan Brocklebank was on the screen again. She was wearing sunglasses.

"Please stand for the pledge," she said.

At that moment, colored lights began to flash. A drum machine started to play. And then Morgan Brocklebank started rapping. . . .

*"I pledge allegiance to the flag,
'cause if I don't it's such a drag.
Flags are red and white and blue.
Why they are I have no clue."*

"She's rapping her own pledge!" shouted
Ms. Cuddy.

"Our beautiful and spacious skies,
Mom and picnics, apple pies.
Dig our amber waves of grain,
Purple mountains, fruited plain.
Broad stripes and bright stars,
Super Bowls and fast cars.
To the republic for which it stands,
Now it's time to all join hands.

"Star-spangled banners wave,
For the free and for the brave.
We pledge allegiance to our flag,
And when we're done we'll go play tag.

"Have a great day at Dirk School!" shouted Morgan Brocklebank.

Ms. Cuddy looked like she was going to explode.

"That Dirk kid did a rap version of the Pledge of Allegiance!" she shouted. "Why didn't *we* think of that?"

A few minutes later Mrs. Patty came in to give us the bad news—eighty people had tuned in to watch the Dirk School announcements. Only sixty had watched ours.

"Nooooooooo!" shouted Ms. Cuddy, falling to her knees. "They beat us *again*!"

"I'll do better next time," I promised.

"I'll have the whole weekend to work on new jokes."

"No more jokes!" Ms. Cuddy shouted as she got up. "Dirk School makes their morning announcements fun and lively. Our show has to be more entertaining. So I have made a big decision. We need to bring in some fresh blood around here."

Fresh blood? Gross! Why would you bring blood to a school?

"If one anchor is good, two anchors would be *twice* as good," Ms. Cuddy said. "So, starting Monday, A.J., we're going to team you up with a co-anchor. And the co-anchor will be . . . Andrea."

WHAT?!

The Worst Day
of My Life

"Thank you thank you thank you!" Andrea said. "I always wanted to be on TV!"

It wasn't fair! Starting the TV station was *my* idea, not Andrea's. I was supposed to be the anchor. This was the worst day of my life.

"Should I write a script for Monday, Ms. Cuddy?" Andrea asked.

"No," she replied. "I chose you to be co-anchor so you and A.J. can banter with each other."

"Banter?" I asked. "What does *that* mean?"

"Just talk to each other," Ms. Cuddy told us. "You two have great chemistry together."

"Ooooo!" Ryan said. "A.J. and Andrea have great chemistry together. They must be in *love!*"

"When are you gonna get married?" asked Michael.

* * *

On Monday there were two chairs at the anchor desk—one for me and one for Little Miss Know-It-All. Andrea was sitting there, getting her nose powdered by Emily. The guys were working with the cameras and stuff.

"Hey, what about *me*?" I shouted. "Aren't you going to powder *my* nose?"

"You told me to leave you alone," Emily replied.

"I want my nose powdered!" I shouted.

"Thirty seconds to airtime!" shouted Alexia.

We were all on pins and needles.

Well, not really. We were sitting on chairs. If we were on pins and needles, it would have hurt.

"Okay, it's go time, folks!" said Ms. Cuddy. "Are my anchors ready?"

"Yeah!" Andrea and I said.

"I can't *hear* you!"

"YEAH!"

"Break a leg out there," said Ms. Cuddy.

What?! Why would she want us to break our legs? That made no sense at all.

"Three . . . two . . . one . . . ," said Alexia. "Action!"

"Welcome to the morning announcements," I said. "My name is A.J. and I hate school."

"My name is Andrea and I *love* school," said Andrea. "Should we start with the weather, Arlo?"

"Sure," I said. "The weather outside is—"

I didn't get the chance to finish my sentence because Andrea interrupted me.

"Instead of talking about *today's* weather," she said, "I'd like to talk about *tomorrow's* weather."

"What?" I asked. "Who cares about tomorrow's weather? We can talk about tomorrow's weather tomorrow."

"Did you say *tomorrow*?" Andrea asked.

That's when she did the most amazing thing in the history of the world. She got up and started *singing*!

"The sun'll come out . . . tomorrow . . ."

Oh no! Andrea was singing that dumb song that she always sings! She threw her arms out to her sides and sang the whole song. It was horrible. After that was over, she sang another song about a hard-knock life or something. I'm not sure of the words because I was covering my ears the whole time. I thought I was gonna die.

Finally, Andrea stopped singing and sat down. She looked at me like it was my turn to start talking.

"Uh, so do we have any birthdays at Ella Mentry School today?" I asked.

"There are no birthdays today, Arlo," Andrea said. "So instead, I'd like to do a little dance."

WHAT?!

Before I could say anything, Andrea had climbed up on the desk and started clog dancing, which is some kind of dance that plumbers do.

Andrea takes clog-dancing lessons after school. In fact, Andrea takes classes in *everything* after school. If they gave classes in nose picking, she would probably take them so she could get better at it.

Finally, Andrea finished her dumb dance and sat back down. Then she looked at me again like I was supposed to say something.

"Lunch for today will be macaroni and—"

"I'm sorry, but that's all the time we have for the announce-ments," Andrea

said. "Have a great day, Ella Mentry students, and we'll see you right here . . . tomorrow."

Then she started singing again.

"I love ya, tomorrow; you're always a day away."

"And . . . cut!" shouted Alexia.

The red light on top of the camera turned off.

"Awesome!" said Ms. Cuddy. "That was fantastic, Andrea! Let's see what those Dirk jerks are doing with *their* morning announcements."

She flipped the channel to the Dirk station. It looked like every kid in Dirk School was out on their playground. They were all singing and dancing, and they were dressed like werewolves.

"WOW!" everybody said, which is "MOM" upside down.

"That's Michael Jackson's 'Thriller'!" Andrea shouted. "I've seen that video!"*

"Nooooooooo!" shouted Ms. Cuddy. "Not 'Thriller'!"

Then she fell on the floor and started sobbing.

---

*"Thriller" is a cool video. You should watch it.

A Word from Our Sponsor

It didn't take long for the bad news to arrive. Our ratings went *down*! Only forty people tuned in to see our morning announcements. *Ninety* people watched Dirk School put on "Thriller."

"This is a disaster!" Ms. Cuddy moaned. "Everything we do, Dirk does better."

I must admit, I was secretly happy that our ratings went down. If Andrea's singing and dancing had been a big hit, we would never have heard the end of it. But Ms. Cuddy was really upset. She looked like her dog had died or something.

"It's okay, Ms. Cuddy," Ryan said. "It doesn't matter to us how many eyeballs we have."

Suddenly, Ms. Cuddy jumped up. She had that fire in her eyes again.

"Well, it matters to *me*!" she shouted. "I'm not a quitter! If at first you don't succeed, try, try again! That's what we do. We *never* give up! Right?"

"Right," we all said.

"I can't *hear* you!"

"RIGHT!"

Ms. Cuddy must have hearing problems or something. She's always saying she can't hear us. She should go to a doctor and get her ears checked.

She paced back and forth for a few minutes, and then she snapped her fingers.

"I've got it!" she said.

Grown-ups always snap their fingers when they have a good idea. Nobody knows why.

"You've got *what*?" we all asked.

"We need to get your parents involved so they'll watch our station instead of the Dirk station!" she said. "And I know just how to do it!"

When we came in the next morning, Ms. Cuddy handed scripts to me and Andrea. Emily powdered our noses. The red light went on. Alexia shouted, "Action!"

"My name is A.J. and I hate school," I said.

"My name is Andrea and I *love* school," said Andrea. "The weather today is chilly. We'll be right back after this message."

The red light went off. We looked up at the TV screen. And you'll never believe in a million hundred years who was on it.

My mother!

"Oh no!" I groaned.

"Hi, I'm A.J.'s mom," my mother said. "I wanted to tell you that I love you, and I'm so proud of you being such a big TV star

and everything. Oh, one more thing, A.J.
Clean your room. It's a pigsty."

"Oh, snap!" said Ryan. "Your mom just
said you were a pig."

The red light went on again. I looked at
my script.

"Today's lunch will be chicken fingers," I read. "We have one birthday today. Darby Dearborn in second grade turns eight years old. And now, a word from our sponsor."

The red light went off. We looked up at the TV screen. And you'll never believe who was on it.

Ryan's mom!

"Oh no!" groaned Ryan.

"Hi everyone," Ryan's mom said. "Kids grow up so fast these days. I can hardly believe my little Ryan is such a big boy now, working for a real TV station. It seems like only yesterday that I was giving him a bath in our kitchen sink."

Everybody looked at Ryan. He was holding his hands in front of his face.

"You took a bath in your sink yesterday?" I asked Ryan.

"No!" Ryan shouted.

"I remember when my baby Ryan was crawling around on all fours," said Ryan's mom. "All he could do was burp and pee and say goo-goo. I had to wipe his little bottom for him. And *now* look at him."

Everybody looked at Ryan. He was still holding his hands over his face.

"Is she finished?" he asked.

"Your mom is weird," I told Ryan.

"She's always going overboard," he said.

"She jumps out of boats?" I asked.

The morning announcements went on forever because we had to watch commercials from everybody's parents. Finally, after we had all been embarrassed, the red light went off. It was over.

"Cut!" shouted Alexia.

"Fantastic!" shouted Ms. Cuddy. "Your parents *had* to watch that. Everybody wants to see themselves on TV."

Sniffing Out Stories

Well, Ms. Cuddy was wrong, because once again our ratings went down and Dirk's went up. They did a version of my favorite show, *Win Money or Eat Bugs*. The Dirk teachers had to answer trivia questions. When they got them right, they won money. When they got them wrong, they had to eat bugs. Even I wanted to see that.

"Noooooooo!" Ms. Cuddy shouted. "Not *again*! We will beat those Dirk dorks! You just wait and see! I'll make them wish they never tangled with me!"

Ms. Cuddy was fuming. She paced back and forth mumbling to herself. Then she snapped her fingers.

"I've got it!" she said.

"You've got *what?*" we all asked.

"I'll tell you tomorrow morning," she said mysteriously.

When we got to the studio the next morning, Ms. Cuddy was waiting outside, but the door was locked.

"Aren't we going to do the announcements today?" Andrea asked.

"We need to change our format," she replied. "We need to get out of the studio and into the streets. That's where the people are. Come on, let's go!"

Ms. Cuddy had a portable TV camera. She led us across the street.

"Where are we going?" Neil asked.

"We're going to follow our noses and sniff out stories," she replied. "We're going to do investigative reporting."

There was just one problem. The streets were empty. All the kids had been dropped off at school. All the parents had left for work or gone home. There was nobody around.

"There are no stories out here," Michael said.

"You just aren't looking hard enough," said Ms. Cuddy. "See, this car is parked too close to a fire hydrant. That's illegal! I'm calling the police!"

"It's like an inch too close," said Alexia.

"Yeah, what's the big deal?" asked Ryan.

Ms. Cuddy ignored us. She pulled out her cell phone and punched in a number.

"Hello, police department?" she said. "We have a crime in progress across the street from Ella Mentry School. Send some cops over right away, and a tow truck too. Hurry!"

A few seconds later we heard a siren. Ms. Cuddy handed the camera to Michael

and told me to stand in front of the car.

"Okay, A.J.," she said. "Action!"

"Uh . . . my name is A.J.," I said, looking into the camera. "I'm standing here across the street from Ella Mentry School, where there appears to be a crime in progress."

At that moment a tow truck and two police cars screeched to a halt next to us. Some cops got out and rushed over. Michael filmed the whole thing.

"What's the problem?" one of the cops said.

"This car is parked illegally," I told him.

He looked at the car.

"It's a few inches too close to the hydrant," he said. "You dragged us over here for *that*?"

The cops looked like they were going to leave.

"People can't just park wherever they want," shouted Ms. Cuddy. "Don't we have laws in this country?"

"Who are *you*?" a cop asked Ms. Cuddy.

"I'm a concerned citizen," she said. "My taxes pay your salary! Criminals need to learn their lesson! Do your job! You've got to tow that car away."

The cop rolled his eyes.

"Okay, boys," he said. "Tow it."

The tow truck driver attached some chains to the car and started towing it down the street. At that moment, Mr. Klutz came out of the school.

"What's going on?" he asked. "Why aren't you using the TV studio we paid a million dollars for?"

"We decided to hit the streets and do some investigative reporting," Ms. Cuddy said.

"Yeah," I told Mr. Klutz. "A car was parked here illegally, so we had the police tow it away."

Mr. Klutz turned around and looked down the street. Then he looked at the empty spot where the car had been.

"Wait a minute," he said. "That was *my* car you towed away!"

"*Your* car?" we all shouted.

"Oops," said Ms. Cuddy.

"Is this some kind of a *joke*?" asked Mr. Klutz.

Of course not. A joke would be, like—*A library is the tallest building in the world, because it has the most stories.* Mr. Klutz totally doesn't know what a joke is. He went running down the street chasing the tow truck.

It was hilarious.

Breaking News

Well, I guess our investigative report didn't attract many eyeballs. Dirk School beat us *again*. They put on a reality show called *Killer Karaoke*. Kids had to sing songs while their classmates dropped water balloons on their heads. I wish I had come up with *that* idea.

Ms. Cuddy looked more depressed than ever. She just sat there with her head in her hands.

"I give up," she said. "I'm out of ideas. No matter *what* we do, those Dirk dorks beat us. I quit."

"What?!" we all shouted.

"You can't quit, Ms. Cuddy!" said Ryan.

"Remember what you told us?" said Andrea. "If at first you don't succeed, try, try again."

"I tried again," moaned Ms. Cuddy. "And *again*. It's no use! We just can't beat those monsters!"

That's when I got the greatest idea in the history of the world.

I asked Ms. Cuddy to give us *one* day before quitting. After school, I held a secret meeting with the gang. I told them my idea. The next morning, we were ready to put it into action.

"Action!" yelled Alexia.

"My name is A.J. and I hate school," I

said into the mic.

"My name is Andrea and I *love* school. Now for the morning announcements. The weather today is—"

A big banner flashed on the screen: **BREAKING NEWS!**

"I'm sorry, Andrea," I said, "but I have to interrupt the morning announcements. We have important news. Monsters have been spotted at Ella Mentry School!"

"What?" Andrea yelled.

At that moment the weirdest thing in the history of the world happened—a zombie ran past the camera!

Well, it *looked* like a zombie. It was actually Neil the nude kid, dressed like a

zombie.* Emily had done a great job on his makeup.

"What was *that*?" Andrea shouted.

"It looked like a zombie to me," I said.

---

*Hey, do you know where zombies go swimming? In the Dead Sea.

Mr. Klutz came running into the studio.

"Was that a zombie?" he shouted.

"It *looked* like a zombie," said Ms. Cuddy.

Mr. Klutz ran in front of the camera.

"Lock the doors!" he shouted. "Nobody gets in or out of the building! Call the police! There's a zombie in our school!"

Then he ran out of the room.

"We repeat," Andrea said, "a zombie has been spotted inside Ella Mentry School. Please remain calm. As soon as we have more information—"

At that moment something even *weirder* happened—a vampire ran past the camera!

Well, it *looked* like a vampire. It was

actually Ryan, dressed like a vampire. He was growling.

"What was *that*?" I shouted.

"It looked like a vampire," said Andrea.

"Zombies and vampires have invaded our school!" I shouted. "Don't panic!"

"Let's go get the story, you guys!" Alexia shouted.

Andrea and I grabbed our mics. Michael grabbed Ms. Cuddy's portable camera. We dashed into the hallway. Kids were spilling out of the classrooms.

"Help!" some kid yelled. "It's a monster attack!"

"The zombies and vampires are taking over!" yelled somebody else.

"I'm too young to die!"

"This is *great*!" said Ms. Cuddy. "Are you getting all this on video, Michael?"

"Run for your lives!" somebody screamed.

In seconds the hallway was jammed with teachers and students running around, yelling and screaming and shrieking and hooting and hollering and freaking out.

"We are reporting the monster attack live!" I shouted into the mic. "We will stay on the air until this crisis is over."

Andrea stuck her microphone in some girl's face and asked her if she had seen any monsters.

"No," the girl replied. "But I heard a rumor that they're mutant alien zombies

from outer space!"

"I heard the zombies kidnapped Mr. Klutz!" some other kid said.

I spotted Officer Spence, our school security guard.

"Have you seen any zombies or vampires?" I asked him.

"Not yet," he replied. "But we can't let those monsters take over the school. We'll track them down."

"You're a real hero, Officer Spence," I told him.

"Just doing my job, A.J."

Everybody was going crazy in the hallways. Somebody screamed. Andrea and I ran around the corner. There was a zombie on the floor, groaning and drooling.

Well, it looked like a zombie. It was actually Neil again.

"Here's one of the zombies now!" Andrea said. "We're going to get an exclusive interview."

I stuck my mic in Neil's face.

"You've been turned into a flesh-eating zombie," I said. "How do you feel?"

"Grrrrrreat!" Neil replied.

"When did you first realize you were a zombie?"

"On Tuesday," Neil said.

"What are you going to do next?"

"Eat the humans," Neil said.

"Good luck with that," Andrea told him.

"Thank you for taking the time to talk with us."

I heard a loud *bang* outside. I looked out the window. A helicopter had landed on the front lawn of the school. A bunch of guys jumped out wearing body armor, gas masks, and other cool stuff.

"Come out with your hands up, monsters!" one of them shouted through a bullhorn.

"The army is here!" Andrea yelled into her mic.

Ms. Cuddy opened the front door so the army guys could come in.

"Where are the monsters?" one of them shouted.

"They went that a-way!" I told them.

"Follow me, men!"

The army guys ran all over the school looking for monsters, but they never found any because Neil and Ryan took off their costumes. After a while the army guys got back in the helicopter and left.

"It appears as though the monster attack is over," Andrea said. "You may return to your classrooms now. Have a great day, Ella Mentry students."

"And . . . cut!" shouted Alexia.

"That was *awesome*!" said Ms. Cuddy.

When the monster attack was over, Mr. Klutz went from class to class to make sure everyone was okay. When he got to our TV studio, we asked him how many people had watched our station and how many people had watched the Dirk School station.

"*Nobody* watched the Dirk station," he told us. "Everybody in town was watching *us.*"

"Yes!" Ms. Cuddy shouted. "Victory is ours! We're number one! We're number one!"

She started dancing all over the room, laughing and yelling and screaming and shrieking and hooting and hollering and generally freaking out.

"Man," Alexia said, "Ms. Cuddy is going overboard."

Why is everybody always talking about boats?

Well, that's pretty much what happened. Maybe the army will find out that the monsters were just kids dressed up like monsters. Maybe Mr. Cooper will stop throwing apples at doctors. Maybe we'll buy a thousand refrigerators and put them in the playground. Maybe they'll get a life on Mars. Maybe everybody will stop thinking in boxes and talking about boats all the time. Maybe we'll rent some eyeballs. Maybe basketball players will stop dribbling all over the floor. Maybe Ms. Cuddy will go to a doctor and get her ears checked. Maybe Andrea will stop singing songs from *Annie* all the time. Maybe those jerky Dirk dorks will stop eating bugs and throwing water balloons at each other. Maybe Ryan will stop taking baths in his kitchen sink. Maybe we can talk Ella Mentry into giving us another million dollars.

But it won't be easy!